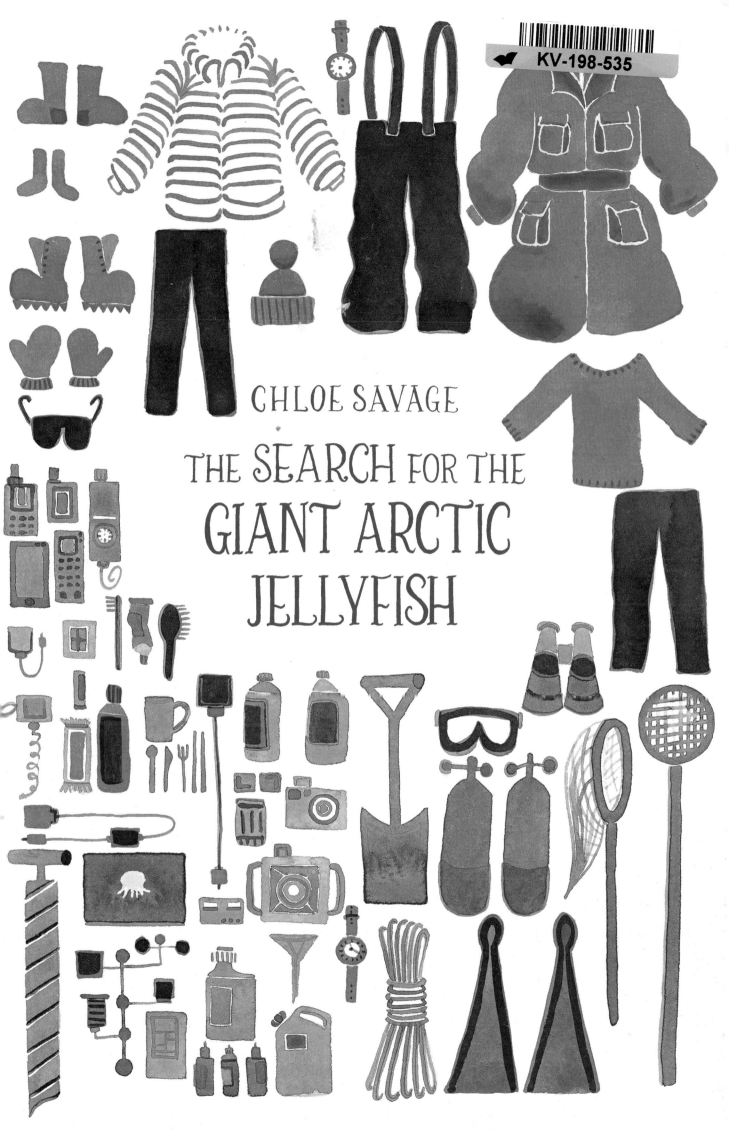

CHLOE SAVAGE

THE SEARCH FOR THE GIANT ARCTIC JELLYFISH

For all my family, the old and the brand new

C. S.

WALKER BOOKS
AND SUBSIDIARIES
LONDON • BOSTON • SYDNEY • AUCKLAND

First published 2022 by Walker Books Ltd, 87 Vauxhall Walk, London SE11 5HJ • This edition published 2023 • ©2022 Chloe Savage • The right of Chloe Savage to be identified as author of this work has been asserted in accordance with the Copyright, Designs and Patents Act 1988 • This book has been typeset in Bodoni Egyptian Pro • Printed in China • All rights reserved. No part of this book may be reproduced, transmitted or stored in an information retrieval system in any form or by any means, graphic, electronic or mechanical, including photocopying, taping and recording, without prior written permission from the publisher. • British Library Cataloguing in Publication Data: a catalogue record for this book is available from the British Library • ISBN 978-1-5295-1287-8 • www.walker.co.uk • 10 9 8 7 6 5 4 3 2 1

Dr Morley absolutely loves jellyfish.

All her life she has been fascinated by the idea of finding
a jellyfish which everyone talks about but no one has
ever seen: the giant Arctic jellyfish.

Her superb crew have helped with years of research and planning. Now, at long last, they can embark on their adventure to the northernmost tip of the world.

It will be months before they enjoy the ease and comfort of home again. But there is no going back now.

Dr Morley is determined that somewhere out in the icy waters, they will find the elusive giant Arctic jellyfish.

They cross into the Arctic Circle with a majestic
pod of narwhals gliding through the water around
them, but no sign of the giant Arctic jellyfish.

Could it be that the narwhals
know where to look?

To help guide their search, Dr Morley leads her team to collect important measurements and scientific samples. Anything that will help them to seek out the giant Arctic jellyfish.

They dive deep beneath the ice, hopeful to catch even a *glimpse* of a tentacle...

The days go by and with great delight
they meet a curious pod of beluga
whales, and yet no sign of the
giant Arctic jellyfish.

Even while freezing blizzards howl,
the scientists never stop searching.
They watch the playful orca frolic
in the snow but there is still not
one single glimpse of the giant
Arctic jellyfish.

Days and weeks go by...

The crew are sure that if they just
try hard enough, look for long enough,
they will succeed in their quest.

The crew work hard for months,

every day exploring somewhere new.

But, as they battle with the brutal cold, the steadfast
crew begin to miss the warm comforts of home.

They wonder, just maybe, is the giant
Arctic jellyfish really just a myth after all?

Despite their doubts, their faith in Dr Morley keeps the team going. In hope, they sail dangerously close to the formidable ice shelf.

Will they ever catch sight of the giant Arctic jellyfish?

And then finally, there's hope! The bright Arctic
sun has made a feast of delicious squidgy algae,
which must be *irresistible* to a jellyfish.

There isn't a moment to lose! Dr Morley dives in.
If she is going to find her jellyfish anywhere,
it will be here. She is sure this is her moment.

But Dr Morley finds nothing.
Absolutely nothing.

All hope for her dream begins to fade
and sink down into the icy sea.

Dr Morley looks around at her exhausted crew.
No one could ask for more.

They have marvelled at the wonders of life in the
Arctic waters, worked so hard, and come so far.

But no one has seen a single solitary peep
of the giant Arctic jellyfish.

She orders the boat to turn around.
It is time to leave her dream behind...

Wait, could that be...